WITHDRAWN

HOLLY KELLER
ROSATA

GREENWILLOW BOOKS
NEW YORK

Watercolor paints and a black pen were used for the full-color art.
The text type is Bernhard Modern BT.

Printed in Singapore by Tien Wah Press

First Edition   10 9 8 7 6 5 4 3 2 1

LIBRARY OF CONGRESS
CATALOGING-IN-PUBLICATION DATA

Keller, Holly.
Rosata / by Holly Keller.
        p.   cm.
Summary: Having found a hat with a bird on it, Camilla names the
bird Rosata and takes the hat everywhere with her until she meets the
new girl next door.
ISBN 0-688-05320-3 (trade).   ISBN 0-688-05321-1 (lib. bdg.)
[1. Hats—Fiction. 2. Friendship—Fiction.] I. Title.
PZ7.K28132Ro   1995   [E]—dc20   94-21916   CIP   AC

For Marjorie

Camilla was sitting by herself on the back steps one morning, counting clouds, when the garbage truck went by.

As the truck turned the corner, a box bounced off the top. The box was round and pink and tied with a faded black ribbon. Camilla picked up the box and took it inside.

"What is that?" Mama asked.

"Don't know," Camilla said, and she went into her room.

Camilla put the box on the floor and untied
the ribbon. There was a lot of crumpled tissue
paper inside, and under that there was an old hat
decorated with velvet flowers and a small bird made
out of real feathers.

Camilla thought the hat was beautiful, and she
put it on the chair next to her bed.

"You're a pretty bird," she said, when she touched
the feathers, "and you live in a nice garden. I will
never throw you away."

Camilla named the bird Rosata, and she talked to her gently every day.

Sometimes Mama came to the door. "You should be outside playing, Camilla," she would say, "not inside talking to a hat."

But Camilla was happy. She liked talking to Rosata.

One morning when Mama woke Camilla to go to school, Camilla said she didn't want to go unless she could take Rosata with her, and Mama said she thought that would be all right.

But when Camilla came into the kitchen wearing the hat, Victor started to laugh and almost choked on his orange juice. Papa quickly covered his face with the newspaper, and Waffles ran under the table and hissed.

"I don't care what you think," Camilla almost shouted. "If I can't wear it, I'm not going."

And everyone was so surprised that nobody said a word.

Camilla wore her hat to school, and after that she wore it everywhere.

"You are really weird," Victor said, and Jenny, who was in Camilla's class, called her a birdbrain. But Camilla didn't care.

When Victor's friend Tony came over to visit, Camilla went into Victor's room to see what they were doing.

"Don't be a pest, Camilla," Victor said. And when Camilla didn't leave, Victor grabbed her hat and tossed it out into the hall. Camilla ran to get it, and Victor slammed the door behind her.

That made Camilla really mad, and Mama made Victor promise he would never do it again.

One rainy afternoon Camilla and Rosata were sitting on the window seat in the living room. Camilla was drawing pictures of Rosata. She heard a noise and looked outside.

"It's a big moving van," Camilla told Rosata, and then she watched as a car pulled up in front of the house next door. A family got out. There was a girl about the size of Camilla, and two black cats.

The next day was Sunday, and Camilla and Rosata went to the corner for ice cream. When they came back, the new girl was sitting on the front steps of her house.

"My name is Teresa," the new girl said. "What's yours?"

"Camilla," Camilla said softly.

"I like the bird on your hat," Teresa said.

"Her name is Rosata," Camilla said a bit louder.

"She's pretty," Teresa said, and Camilla let Teresa touch Rosata's feathers.

Camilla and Teresa sat outside together and talked until dinnertime.

Camilla and Teresa started playing together every day after school. Once when Camilla stayed overnight at Teresa's house and Teresa's mother took them to the movies, they were just sitting down when Camilla realized she had forgotten her hat.

"Oh, Rosata!" she gasped.

"Don't worry," Teresa whispered. "Rosata will be fine, and you can explain to her tomorrow."

"I will never leave you home again," Camilla promised Rosata the next morning.

But on Halloween Camilla decided to dress up like a witch.

Victor laughed when he saw her. "You can't be a witch in a hat like that," he said.

Camilla looked in the mirror for a long time. She heard Teresa calling from the street, "Come on, Camilla. We'll miss all the good candy!"

"Okay, okay, I'm coming!" Camilla called back.
She put Rosata back on the chair very carefully.
"You probably wouldn't have fun anyway," she
whispered. Then she plopped the witch hat onto
her head, grabbed her pumpkin, and ran outside.

The next week Camilla told Mama that Rosata had a cold and had to stay inside for a few days. And she told Teresa that Rosata stayed home sometimes just because she wanted to.

"She was pretty old when I found her," Camilla said, "and now she's *really* old, and she just can't be going out to play all the time."

"Right," Teresa said.

"Of course, I still talk to her every night before I go to bed," Camilla added, "except maybe when I'm very, very tired."

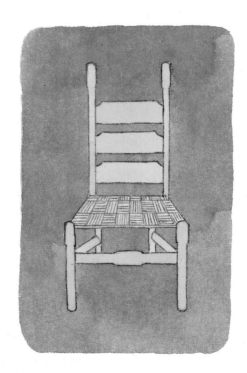

One afternoon Camilla looked for Rosata and couldn't find her anywhere. Mama came into Camilla's room to help look. She took everything off Camilla's chair, and there, at the very bottom of the pile, was the hat.

"Oh," Camilla said, "I guess I forgot where I put it."

Mama cleared off a space on the top of the bookcase. She put the hat right in the middle.

Camilla looked up at Rosata. She looked the same as always.

"I think she'll be happy there," Mama said, "and you will always know where she is."

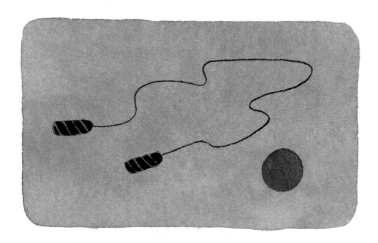

Camilla nodded, but she didn't say anything.
Then she kissed Mama good-bye and went over
to Teresa's.